THE *Miseducation* OF *Ms. G*

THE *Miseducation* OF *Ms. G*

Krystal Grant

Also by Krystal Grant
Under the Palmetto Tree: A Novel

The Miseducation of Ms. G

Krystal Grant

F I R S T   E D I T I O N

ISBN: 978-1-939288-50-9
Library of Congress Control Number: 2014933429

Published by Kenely Books, An Imprint of Wyatt-MacKenzie
kenely@wyattmackenzie.com

For Rodney,

Madison, Collin, and Chase,

James and Okla Kenely,

Cheryl, Terri, Jamilia, and Kayela

I

A GUST OF WIND BLEW UP MS. GREENLEY'S SKIRT exposing her thighs. Two students. Freshmen. Female. Laughed uncontrollably as they caught a glimpse of her black panties. Ms. Greenley quickened her pace down the sidewalk toward her classroom as she held her skirt down with her left hand and clinched her purse with her right. She was embarrassed. Angry.

It was the beginning of the week. Monday mornings always proved to be difficult. But this Monday would be even more challenging due to the 5 day fall vacation the school district had the prior week. No one wanted to be there—not the principal, the students, nor Ms. Greenley.

The 9th grade academy was a hub of activity. The freshman class of Stonedale High School moved through the hallways avoiding teachers, gathering books, and slamming lockers. The warning bell sounded which gave students exactly one minute to get to their designated classes. Ms. Greenley stood at her door greeting her first period students as they made their way into her room. The next ninety minutes would be the best part of Ms. Greenley's day. She taught honors literature to a group of sixteen freshmen who were academically advanced. They were excited about learning. And she was excited to teach them. The class spent the period in collaborative groups reenacting Act III Scene 1 of *The Tragedy of Romeo and Juliet*. After rousing performances the students discussed the similarities and differences between Tybalt and Mercutio, Ms. Greenley's favorite characters.

The teacher walked around the class observing her students and listening in on their in-depth analyses of the play. She was intrigued and quite impressed with the high level of thinking her students displayed. As the period drew to a close beads of sweat formed on Ms. Greenley's forehead and her side began to ache. She watched her honors students pack their books in anticipation of the bell which would allow them to exit her room. She longed for them to stay. This was by far her least challenging class. This was the only time during the day that she was able to make it through a complete lesson. This was her only class that was receptive to learning and actually had a measurable understanding of the concepts she presented. But her second period class was a direct opposite entity all together. This class, her lowest performing, was a group of thirty-nine freshman who failed the previous year's CRCT. Yet, managed to make their way into high school.

Most students in Ms. Greenley's second period class were on a fourth or fifth grade reading level. Twelve of the students were flagged for special education services. Three of them were homeless. And two students only showed up for class once a week (Ms. Greenley had not bothered to find out where they went the remainder of the week). The bell sounded and her honors literature class filed out of the room with little noise.

The pain in Ms. Greenley's side worsened. Her breathing became labored as she anticipated the hell she was about to experience. She picked up a few stray papers that had found their way to the floor and turned on the classroom TV. Channel One, the national news show for high schoolers, would begin shortly after the bell sounded.

Enrique sauntered into the room with his green notebook in hand, pen tucked behind his ear, and an exorbitant amount of gel shaping his hair. He smiled and said in the best English he could, " Hi, Miss." Enrique could never manage to pronounce

Ms. Greenley's name. He simply called her *Miss*. Ms. Greenley smiled and continued fumbling with the television channels. Without turning around she asked Enrique the same question she asked him every single day.

"Where's your textbook?"

Enrique slapped himself on the forehead, pulled his sagging pants up on his waist, and jogged out of the room towards his locker.

For the entire second period Ms. Greenley stood in the center of her room and talked. She was forced to give this group of students direct, whole class instruction. They were unable to work in collaborative groups. Their attention span was too short and their behavior was intolerable. Even though her weekly lesson plans stated that the students would read a section from *The Odyssey* and analyze Odysseus' heroic characteristics using details from the poem, she knew they would not be able to adequately complete the task. So instead, she read "The Cyclops" aloud to her students (because most of the class did not have their textbooks). Then she stood at the Promethean board and wrote notes that the students copied.

It was a typical second period: throngs of students showing up late with no hall pass, paper being thrown about the floor, profanity, texting, and sleeping. Nine students were absent during the class and out of the thirty that were present, only ten of them had their needed materials. Luckily, three students managed to turn in their homework assignment so Ms. Greenley refrained from her usual speech about responsibility and the importance of education.

At precisely 11:15 am, twenty minutes before the end of the class, Jhamario jumped into the room and performed a forward head roll onto the floor. The class exploded in laughter. Just as quickly as he made it to the floor, he was up on his feet with his hands in the air posing like Gabby Douglass in the Olympic Games. A few students congratulated Jhamario's fete with applause. Ms. Greenley, amazed by his acrobatics, immediately scolded Jhamario for his disruption. He crumpled his hall pass into a ball and threw it at Ms. Greenley's face.

"Mark me present, Bitch!" Jhamario pulled his pants up to his waist and walked back out of the room. A sphere of anger crawled into Ms. Greenley's spirit as she bit her bottom lip. She walked over to her computer and began filling out the electronic discipline referral that would be sent to the assistant principal.

Hiding her fury, the teacher waltzed back to her Promethean board and continued describing the details of how Polyphemus ate Odysseus' men in the cave.

II

Mr. Tarver drove down the highway to Stonedale High School at a minimum speed. He was in no rush to get back to work. The assistant principal knew what was waiting for him in his office: piles of discipline referrals, numerous teacher complaints and more that a few disgruntled parents. He took a sip of his coffee and leaned his head on his car seat awaiting the traffic light to change. Mr. Tarver had spent all morning at the Dent County Department of Juvenile Justice. He testified on behalf of his school system in a case against one of his students, Victoria Holden.

Victoria was a sophomore at Stonedale; a beautiful young girl who spent far too much time bullying fellow students and skipping classes. Earlier that year, after four suspensions had been recorded in her file,

Victoria was caught in "the cut" by Mr. Tarver. *The cut*, as the students called it, was a path in the woods behind the school that connected Stonedale High to the adjacent elementary school. The students would skip class and adjourn in the cut to smoke weed and have sex.

When Mr. Tarver found Victoria she was on her knees pleasuring her boyfriend Jelani who was leaning against a tree, grabbing the back of Victoria's head. It was a terrible sight. And Mr. Tarver was sick to his stomach. He yelled at both students to stop what they were doing and charged at them in a rage. Jelani, with his pants still around his ankles, met Mr. Tarver with a fist to his jaw. Mr. Tarver threw the boy in the bushes and grabbed Victoria by the arm, lifting her off the ground. With his free hand, the assistant principal attempted to pull Jelani from the bushes but his strength gave way as Victoria sunk her teeth into his shoulder. She threw her nails into his face and began kicking him. Jelani jumped up from the bushes and joined Victoria in her attack of the assistant principal. After they both tired the couple ran off, through the cut and down Memorial Drive where they hopped on a Marta bus and were not seen for hours.

Back in his office, Mr. Tarver listened as his secretary told him of the myriad of calls he missed while in court. He threw his paperwork on his desk and began typing an email to the school's Principal alerting her that Victoria, along with Jelani had been expelled from school and each sentenced to ten days in the juvenile detention center for simple assault.

A message popped up on Mr. Tarver's computer notifying him that a new discipline referral had arrived in his inbox. It was from Ms. Greenley. The assistant principal raised his eyes in shock. Ms. Greenley never sent referrals to the office. She had always managed to have complete control over her classes and usually handled her discipline without the help of the administration. He knew this must be something serious. Just as he hovered his mouse over the message to open it, the bell sounded for third period signifying the beginning of Mr. Tarver's lunch duty.

❧

Students rushed through the halls and made their way to various lunch lines. On today's menu: fried chicken, macaroni and cheese, green beans, a roll and fruit cup. Mr. Tarver, along with the other administrative staff members, monitored the students and kept order in the overcrowded cafeteria. Mr. Tarver stuffed his hands in his pockets and stood authoritatively beside the vending machines.

He was a large man. Nearly 6'2" and over 220 lbs of lean muscle. Mr. Tarver had worked in education for eight years. He was a former PE teacher who got the job as assistant principal in charge of discipline at Stonedale High three years prior. Mr. Tarver had spent his college career at South Carolina State University breaking records on the football field in hopes of making it into the NFL draft. His hard work paid off. He was a second round draft pick and signed a contract with the Miami Dolphins. But tragedy struck during the first game of his NFL career. In the third quarter of a game against the New Orleans Saints, Tarver sacked the Saints quarterback, injuring his neck. He would never play football again. He remained a member of the Dolphins until the end of that season. But since team doctors told him that another blow to his neck would be fatal, he was released from his contract and he moved back home to begin his teaching career.

Kobe Myers brushed against Mr. Tarver's back and laughed. "What's up, Mr. Tarver?" Kobe asked with a smile.

"Nothing, man. How you doin?"

"It's breezy, Mr. T. It's breezy." Kobe inserted his quarters into the vending machine and retrieved his drink. Mr. Tarver watched Kobe and his friends as they walked to a table in the middle of the lunch room and sat.

"Mr. Tarver, please report to Dr. Moynihan's office". The sound blared through the walkie-talkie that was attached to his hip. Tarver quickly turned and headed towards the school's front office. Dr. Moynihan stood at the desk in the front office giving instructions to the school's secretary. Mr. Tarver waited to be recognized. Once Dr. Moynihan finished her directions, she looked up, gave her assistant principal a stern look and said, "Come with me, Tarver."

He immediately followed his boss into her office. Dr. Moynihan's work space was dimly lit. She normally kept the overhead lights off with only a few lamps lighting the area. Her walls were purple. Shortly after she became principal she'd ordered the custodians to paint her office in her favorite color. There were purple flowers on her desk and the chairs were decorated with purple throw pillows. She wore a purple pendant around her neck. Standing in Dr. Moynihan's office was Officer Bellows, the school's policeman, and Micah Wynbush, a seventeen-year-old junior at the school. Micah's nose was bloody and his eyes were red. There was dirt and grass covering his hair and his clothes were torn. Micah looked down at the floor and shifted his feet while Dr. Moynihan stared at him with pity.

Micah was found walking along Central Avenue during second period. When Officer Bellows approached him, Micah explained that a group of boys jumped on him, dragged him into a parking lot behind a gas station and beat him with bricks and a rusted pipe. Officer Bellows brought Micah back to school and filed a police report. Mr. Tarver's job was to find the boys who were reportedly responsible for the attack. He had their names. Now, Tarver needed to check their schedules to find out if they were in class.

III

Ms. Greenley navigated through the desks in her classroom preparing her students for a reading of Edgar Allan Poe's "The Raven". It was the middle of October, shortly before Halloween and a good time to begin a unit on the author.

The groups began work on a KWL chart then reconvened as a class to discuss what they "know" and what they "want to know" about Poe. Bernard Daly sat in the back of the room slouched in his desk with his hoodie covering his head. His eyes were closed and his cheek rested on his dirty fist. Ms. Greenley called on Bernard to begin reading a short bio of Edgar Alan Poe from his textbook, but he didn't respond. She moved closer to the student and called on him again. Still he didn't respond. Ms. Greenley walked towards Bernard and gently pulled the hoodie from his head. He opened one eye, glared at Ms. Greenley and adjusted the headphones that were in his ears. Bernard pulled the hoodie back over his head and closed his eyes, paying no attention to his instructor. Just as the teacher began to ask Bernard to remove the ear phones from his ears she heard a key unlocking her classroom door. Mr. Tarver walked in with a clip board and his walkie talkie. "Ms. Greenley, please excuse me. I need to see Bernard Daly." She turned to Bernard and pulled the hoodie off of his head.

"Damn, Ms. G, leave me alone!" Bernard said with a mixture of frustration and fear.

"Come with me, young man. And you watch your mouth. Don't you ever talk to an adult that way!" Mr. Tarver's voice was stern and loud. He clenched his fists and watched the boy rise from his seat.

Once Mr. Tarver left with the culprit Ms. Greenley called on another student to read the bio of Edgar Alan Poe from the textbook. She breathed a sigh of relief and tried to keep her composure. Once the biography was read the students turned their attention to the Promethean board in the front of the room as Ms. Greenley showed an episode of The Simpsons. It was the Halloween special from years prior. The cartoon reenacted "The Raven" with James Earl Jones narrating the poem. The students loved it. This was a great way to incorporate technology into her lesson and she knew it would keep her students engaged. Even her most challenging students were attentive while watching the beloved cartoon.

Once the show ended the class read the poem aloud then broke into groups to analyze the various literary devices Poe used. Each student had a chart with the words *alliteration, simile, metaphor, rhyme, onomatopoeia,* and *repetition* written across the top. The groups had to identify the use of each type from the poem. As the students worked Ms. Greenley stood at her podium and quietly read over her lesson plans. Her feet hurt. She slipped off her shoes and let her toes sink into the small carpet that lay on her floor.

Just before the sound of the bell which would end the period, Zenobia raised her hand. "Yes, ma'am?" Ms. Greenley responded. "Bernard left his book bag on the floor". Zenobia pointed towards the back of the room at a green book bag that sat amid a small pile of dirt and trash. "Zenobia, take it to Mr. Tarver's office, please." The girl stood and stretched, exposing her belly button which was decorated with a silver earring. She walked to the back of the room and bent over to grab the bag. Just as Zenobia slung it around her arm onto her back a red brick fell out of the bag. Everyone jumped in shock at the sound. Zenobia looked at Ms. Greenley with confusion on her face.

"Just leave it all there, Zenobia. I'll handle it".

The bell sounded. Students gathered their things and exited the room. Ms. Greenley breathed a heavy sigh and wondered why Bernard would be carrying a brick in his book bag. She called Mr. Tarver's office from her classroom phone and alerted him of the discovery.

"You have got to be kidding me!" was his response. "Just leave it right where you found it. I'll be there in a minute." Ms. Greenley had no idea what was going on but she knew it couldn't be good. Officer Bellows entered her room a short time later and asked to see the brick. Ms. Greenley pointed to the evidence still laying on the floor, along with Bernard's green book bag. Officer Bellows thanked Ms. Greenley and asked her to write a statement relaying the information.

Much to her chagrin, the teacher spent her entire lunch period in Officer Bellows office writing out the statement concerning Bernard Daly and his behavior throughout her class. She included every detail she could remember, from the headphones, to the dirty fist. She divulged each bit of information she could think of. When the statement was handed over to the resource officer Ms. Greenley rushed towards the cafeteria in hopes of grabbing any food that was left in the lunch lines.

"You made it just in time" laughed Mr. McManus,

the head cook. Ms. Greenley thanked him repeatedly as he piled macaroni and green beans on her styrofoam tray.

"White meat or dark?" he asked with a smile.

"White, please." Ms. Greenley said shyly. McManus turned towards the kitchen and wobbled to the large warmer that housed a few leftover trays of chicken. He pulled out two pieces of white meat and placed them neatly on Ms. Greenley's tray. McManus moved his robust body back to the serving line and stretched out his arms. Ms. Greenley took the food. "Thanks." she said as she backed away from him. Mr. McManus continued to smile as he waved goodbye to the woman he thought to be beautiful.

A slight hunger headache crept into Ms. Greenley's skull. She sat at her desk massaging her temples as she waited for her food to cool. She took a bite of her macaroni and was stunned at its temperature. It was steaming. Ms. Greenley opened her mouth and breathed heavily in an attempt to reduce the heat. Her eyes watered as she quickly swallowed the macaroni. It burned her throat. She took a long drink of Coca Cola and was relieved as the liquid cooled her insides.

Ms. Greenley relished in the quiet of her classroom. It was fourth period; the time on her schedule where she created her lessons for the upcoming week. All teachers at her school longed for fourth period planning and she was lucky to have it. For the next ninety minutes Ms. Greenley would be undisturbed by students and unnecessary noise. Her classroom door was locked and she sat with the lights dimmed finishing her lunch.

IV

Lionel Superion moved through the ninth grade academy with ease. He carried with him a dirty broom and ragged dust pan. He had a black trash bag tied around his head. Lionel belted out an old Bob Marley tune as the students stared in amusement.

Buffalo soldier
Dreadlock rasta
Fighting on arrival
Fighting for survival

Lionel sang this tune as he cleaned a social studies classroom after school. As one of the school's custodians, Lionel was responsible for cleaning the ninth grade academy, the library, and the freshman computer lab. He was a sight to see; a fun-loving

Jamaican who spent most of his life on stage entertaining crowds. He was a singer. Since birth Lionel had traveled around Jamaica, the Caribbean and the Americas with his parents who were the founders of the reggae band Dread Head Dancehall Kings. When they weren't touring Lionel spent an exorbitant amount of time in the studio with his father smoking marijuana and creating new music.

This did not leave much time for school. His parents hired a personal tutor when Lionel turned six but the frequency of his lessons diminished once his father began an affair with his instructor. That eight year affair produced two children- Lionel's siblings. At the age of fourteen Lionel dropped out of school altogether and created a reggae band with children of the musicians from the Dread Head Dance Hall Kings. Lionel's band was legendary. They were called The Rum Runners and they enjoyed the same amount of success as their parents. In twelve years time The Rum Runners produced five chart-topping albums. They performed for leaders around the world, graced the covers of Time and Newsweek Magazines, and were interviewed by everyone from Oprah Winfrey to Chris Wallace.

During a performance at the Atlantis Resort in the Bahamas Lionel's drummer, Muta "Styx" Martin suffered a violent seizure. Styx was transported to Princess Margaret Hospital in Centerville, Nassau .

He slipped into a coma and died three days later. The Rum Runners were devastated. Plagued by complicated grief Lionel began seeing a therapist in Kingston. He was diagnosed with anxiety and severe depression. His therapist prescribed him with Lexapro and monitored Lionel closely while taking the drug.

By the time Lionel was thirty five years old, he found himself homeless and penniless. He had squandered all his millions by purchasing illegal amounts of Lexapro and any other anti depressant he could find. Lionel moved to the states once he sobered and had been working as a custodian ever since.

Old pirates, yes dey rob I
Sold I to the merchant ships
Minutes after dey took I
From the bottomless pit
But my hand was made strong
By de hand of de Almighty
We forward in this generation
Triumphantly
Won't you help to sing......Redemption song!

Lionel emptied the trash in Mr. Al-Hamin's classroom and swept the floor while singing his favorite Bob Marley song. He danced with the broom as if it were a woman. Mr. Al-Hamin paid no attention to the custodian. All of the staff members were accustomed to Lionel's behavior and accepted him as one of their own. With the trash bag still tied around his head Lionel yelled out a sentence or two to Mr. Al-Hamin and waved his hand goodbye. Al-Hamin waved, not understanding Lionel's strong Jamaican accent.

"See ya lata, Jamaica!" Al-Hamin shouted. Jamaica. This is what everyone at Stonedale High School called him. No one knew his real name and no one seemed to care. Jamaica was sufficient.

Lionel pushed his large trashcan to the adjacent classroom where Ms. Greenley was seated at her desk. She typed vigorously on her computer and squinted her eyes at the screen. Her classroom was neatly organized and not much trash was strewn about. She had used part of her planning period to clean the room.

"Hello, preddy lady!" Jamaica called out.

Ms. Greenley laughed at his greeting and told him hello.

Jamaica began rambling in his heavy accent about two students who broke into his car the day before. He grew increasingly angry as he told his tale. Ms. Greenley responded with an "ah ha" and "really?" but she could barely make out what he said. Jamaica's accent was heavy. Very heavy.

Ms. Greenley printed the document she'd been typing and shut down her computer. As she exited the room Jamaica gazed at her with a smile, exposing his gold tooth. "You sure are uh preddy gurl," he said longingly . "You should come bak to Jamaica wit me." "It's too hot in Jamaica!" Ms. Greenley said quickly as she continued walking out of the room. Lionel was crushed.

The Jamaican wiped each of the desks with pine cleaner and swept her floor. He always took special care of Ms. Greenley's room. He loved her. Well, lusted her, would be more appropriate. Jamaica had had his share of women while touring with The Rum Runners so he was no novice to getting a woman's attention. But he had grown old. His excessive alcohol use degenerated his body at a fast pace. And the drugs did nothing to help his mental state. Of course, the trash bag around his head didn't help much either.

Jamaica picked up a pen from Ms. Greenley's desk and pulled a pink laminated hall pass from his trashcan. He sat at a student's desk and inhaled the smell of pine. Jamaica wrote:

You an me us neva part
We come to mi hom Jamaica
And dere we stay.
I make you me queen.

He stuck the love letter on Ms. Greenley's keyboard and pushed his large trashcan out of the door and down the hall singing another Bob Marley tune.

V

THE EMERGENCY STAFF MEETING WAS HELD IN the auditorium. 642 seats decorated in red fabric surrounded a theatrical stage. A large painting of a pirate was displayed on the ceiling amid the stage lights. Staff members filed in as Dr. Moynihan and Mr. Tarver talked secretively beside the stage. Teachers and staff members sauntered into the auditorium and took their seats. Some graded papers, others sent texts and some sat pondering the reason for the meeting.

Dr. Moynihan called everyone to attention and thanked them for coming. She apologized for any inconveniences and promised that the meeting would brief. The principal explained that there were certain developments at the county office that the teachers needed to be aware of. Dent County School

System's superintendent, Dr. Dagen, was found in his home earlier that morning with a gunshot wound to his head. He had committed suicide.

The staff was stunned. Some teachers gasps while others hung their heads in sadness. Others rose from their seats in disbelief.

" I'm sure you'll hear about it on the news once you get home." Dr. Moynihan said in a shaky voice. "If you're contacted by any reporters, the County asks that you not make any kind of statement. Finally, do not discuss this with your students." Try to have a good afternoon and I'll see you all tomorrow."

The staff of Stonedale High School did not move. They waited for an explanation. They waited for someone to make sense of what they heard. No one did.

That evening, all the local news stations were consumed with reports about the Superintendent's death. They reported that Dr. Dagen and his wife had argued the previous night about an extramarital affair. Mrs. Dagen found several inappropriate text messages between her husband and a woman named Vonetta Charles, the district's Chief Financial Officer. Mrs. Dagen demanded answers. When her husband refused to deliver a satisfactory response she began threatening to expose his grand misuse of county funds–their annual trip to Hawaii, the Rolex watches, the secret bank account, the numerous home renovations, all of which were paid for with County money. He slapped her and they fought. In a total rage Dr. Dagen grabbed his handgun from its case in the master closet of their home and beat his wife with it. He stared at Mrs. Dagen's unconscious body on their bedroom floor. Stunned at the terrible turn of events, Dr. Dagen called 911, reported that there had been an accident, then turned the gun on himself. Mrs. Dagen was admitted to the hospital with a concussion and broken ear drum. After her condition stabled, she gave the police an account of what occurred .

By the time Thanksgiving break ended Vonetta Charles had been fired, several Dekalb County board members were suspended and the Dent County district attorney had announced his plan to bring criminal charges against the CFO and her assistant for gross mismanagement of county funds, forgery, coercion, and theft.

❧

It was early December. The ninth grade students had one week to ready themselves for their End of Course Tests. The school district placed heavy emphasis on the success of this test and used the scores to measure the teachers' effectiveness and the students' learning. Ms. Greenley's second period class sat in their desks with their winter coats buttoned tightly, hats on their heads, and scarves around their necks. Some students blew air into their closed fists to heat their hands. Ms. Greenley stacked the EOCT practice packet on the table and explained to the students that they should work on them quietly. She then called the students up row by row to retrieve a packet.

Ms. Greenley wore green gloves. A matching green scarf hung loosely around her neck and cascaded down her back almost touching the floor. The room was freezing. Ms. Greenley tried her best to ignore the temperature. For the past three days the heat in the ninth grade academy wing of the building was broken. The temperature on the thermostat read 47 degrees and was steadily dropping. Ms. Greenley walked around her room monitoring the student's progress and giving assistance when needed.

"Enrique, put your phone away." Ms. Greenley said quietly.

"Yes, miss." he responded as he finished the text message and stuffed his cell phone in his pocket.

The loud speaker in Ms. Greenley's classroom began beeping, signifying an impending announcement from the office. "Please pardon this interruption." blared Mr. Tarver. "All ninth grade students, please report to the gymnasium. Ninth grade academy teachers, stand in the hall ways to ensure that each student moves swiftly and orderly. Thank you." Ms. Greenley's class jumped up without notice and scrambled out of the room leaving their belongings strewn about the floor.

The assembly would last the remainder of the period. Dr. Fonroy, Stonedale High's assistant principal over testing, gave the students information about next week's schedule changes due to the End of Course Test administration. Victor Collins sat at the top of the bleachers. He was a sophomore at the school and had no business in the assembly. Victor was skipping math class that day because he decided that he hated his teacher, Mr. Parmuth. The previous day, Victor sat in the back of his Algebra II class eating a box of Krispy Kreme doughnuts. Mr. Parmuth told Victor several times to put the box away. But this was Victor's first meal since eating school lunch the day before and he was starving. Mr. Parmuth walked to the back of the class and snatched the box from Victor's hands then threw it in the garbage. With doughnut glaze stuck to his chin Victor jumped up in a rage and pushed Mr. Parmuth from behind, knocking him to the floor. Victor retrieved his doughnuts from the trash and ran out the door. That night, Victor slept on a bench at the Marta bus station. He knew he was in big trouble but the hunger pangs he felt overtook his thoughts.

Not having anywhere else to go, Victor walked back to school that next morning. It was cold. And he knew being at school was better than being exposed to the freezing temperatures. He did everything he could to avoid Dr. Moynihan, Mr. Tarver, and Mr. Parmuth.

Dr. Fonroy finished his speech and turned the assembly over to Ms. Crossfield, the head counselor. She gave the students information about an upcoming field trip to Clark Atlanta University, a local historically black college. While Ms. Crossfield talked, Dr. Fonroy walked over to Officer Bellows who was standing at the gymnasium entrance with his hands on his belt. Bellows bent down as Dr. Fonroy whispered in his ear.

The assembly concluded at the ringing of the bell. All students filed out of the gym in their normal disorderly fashion. Just as Victor walked through the exit, Officer Bellows grabbed his arm and said, "Come with me, son".

VI

The two-week Christmas break was a much needed vacation for Ms. Greenley and the other staff members of Stonedale High School. But the joy of their winter holidays quickly vanished as they headed back to work to begin a new semester. Ms. Greenley went over her class syllabus with the new group of students in her first period. After the semester was briefly outlined and all questions answered, the class read the short story "Thank you, Ma'm" by Langston Hughes. This was not a part of the curriculum, but in years past it had proven to hold the student's attention. The class read the story aloud then responded to a few questions about the characters, plot, setting and theme. Ms. Greenley then passed out white art paper to each of her students and instructed them to illustrate a scene from the story.

The student's drawings were comical. It was amusing to see how they imagined Luella Bates Washington Jones and Roger, the story's characters. Ms. Greenley found it odd that these teenagers would find such joy in activities that a kindergartener would appreciate. But her students loved to color. They would remain quiet for most of the class period, intently focused on their masterpieces. Then they'd proudly hold up their creations for the class to approve.

By the end of the week Ms. Greenley had memorized most of her students names. She read through the numerous IEP's she was responsible for and developed a modified instruction for each of the special needs students. It was a headache, but it was a necessary part of her job.

Each of her classes had been assigned a research paper on an American author. Ms. Greenley instructed her students to meet her in the computer lab on the science hall to work on their essays. While the students looked up information on Zora Neale Hurston, James Baldwin, William Wadsworth, and a host of other authors, Ms. Greenley walked around the room monitoring the student's progress and clarifying any misunderstandings. Just as she bent down to remove a pencil from the floor the fire alarm blared through the halls. Students jumped up from each corner of the room and ran out of the computer lab. Frustrated with the disturbance, Ms. Greenley grabbed her attendance book and slowly walked out of the room. Dr. Fonroy stood in the hallway beside his office directing students out the doors of the school towards the baseball field. It was mass confusion. Three thousand students against one hundred sixty staff members. Dr. Fonroy smiled and nodded his head as Ms. Greenley passed. She waved and continued moving with the crowd. Just as Ms. Greenley pushed the doors open to exit the building she heard fireworks go off in the side parking lot. A few students screamed and others began to run. A rush of children raced passed Ms. Greenley back into the building. The fireworks continued as students ran for cover, hid behind cars, and disappeared into the woods. Zenobia, Ms. Greenley's student from the previous semester lay on the ground shaking. She had blood spilling from her arm and sweat pouring down her face. Zenobia had been shot.

As Ms. Greenley turned to go back into the building for help she saw T-Dog, her student from the preceding year. T-Dog walked towards the building carrying a 9 mm pistol. Ms. Greenley froze in fear. She was paralyzed. T-Dog (whose real name was Antonio) looked past Ms. Greenley with madness in his eyes.

"Tony what are you doing?" she said in a shaky voice.

T-Dog did not respond. He flung the doors of the school open and walked in. Dr. Fonroy met T-Dog at the door. Before the assistant principal could say anything T-Dog shot at him twice. The bullets hit Dr. Fonroy in his chest and he fell to the floor in a slump. Ms. Greenley screamed. She looked around for help. There were students still hiding behind cars in the parking lot. She yelled for someone to call 911 as she ran back to the spot where her student lay. Zenobia had stopped shaking. There were no more beads of sweat forming on her face. She was still. Ms. Greenley put her hand on Zenobia's chest. There was no heartbeat. Zenobia was not breathing. She was dead.

Ms. Greenley called out to Jesus and began to cry. She screamed in terror at what she witnessed. Not knowing what to do she rushed back into the entrance of the building where Dr. Fonroy had fallen. His shirt was soaked with blood and his glasses lay sideways on his face. Ms. Greenley straightened his glasses and called his name. Dr. Fonroy did not move.

Ms. Greenley heard another round of gunshots coming from the cafeteria and more people screaming. She reached in Dr. Fonroy's pocket for his cell phone. With bloody, quivering hands she managed to dial 911 and report what had happened.

The 911 operator spoke quickly. "We are aware of the situation and have patrolmen and medical services en route. Please stay on the line until you hear police sirens." Ms. Greenley knelt beside Dr. Fonroy's dead body and told the emergency worker all that she saw. She described the shooter and told of Zenobia and her assistant principal's deaths. As the operator tried to calm Ms. Greenley, the teacher looked down the long hallway towards the computer lab where her students sat a few moments ago completing their essays.

There was T-Dog. He marched towards Ms. Greenley dragging Stormy Marshall behind him. Stormy was a senior at Stonedale High School. She was homecoming queen, a cheerleader, and president of her school's National Honor Society. Just that morning Stormy has rushed into Ms. Greenley's room to show her the acceptance letter she received from Tuskegee University. Stormy wanted to be a dentist. She planned to go to Tuskegee, major in Biology, then attend Howard University's School of Medicine to earn her DDS. Ms. Greenley was proud. Stormy had always been a kind, hardworking girl who was focused on her studies. The teacher had written a stellar letter of recommendation for Stomy. She could not understand T-Dog's rage towards the girl.

Looking up at T-Dog, Ms. Greenley dropped the cell phone in shock. The 911 operator continued talking as Ms. Greenley stood in fear for her life. Stormy was screaming furiously, trying to break free from T-Dog's grip. As he approached Ms. Greenley she looked down at his gun. Very quietly Ms. Greenley said, "Tony, please stop".

T-Dog had tears in his eyes. He looked at Ms. Greenley and said, "You betta move. You know I don't wanna hurt you Ms. G; but I will. You see what I did to Dr. Fonroy!" T-Dog pointed towards the assistant principal with his gun. Ms. Greenley looked at Dr. Fonroy's bleeding body. A pool of blood had gathered around her feet.

"What are you gonna do with Stormy?" Ms. Greenley asked.

"Imma beat her ass!" Antonio yelled.

Stormy screamed for T-Dog to let her go. She twisted and turned but could not break free from his hold.

T-Dogs dreadlocks cascaded down his back. He had a perfectly shaped nose and perfect teeth. He was a smart boy but was plagued with many problems at home. His mother was dead so T-Dog was forced to live with his grandmother. Last year, Ms. Janie, T-Dogs grandmother, had fallen ill. Because of her sickness T-Dog began to miss an enumerable amount of school days. He spent most of his time at the hospital sitting by her side. Ms. Greenley visited Ms. Janie in the hospital on two occasions. She took flowers and magazines for the woman to read. T-Dog was thrilled to see Ms. Greenley show such kindness. On the days that he made it to school, he'd spend his time in the back of Ms. Greenley's class on the computer. He did not like school. But Ms. Greenley's class was a safe haven for him. She was one of the few teachers he could talk to. Ms. Greenley made an extra effort to help T-Dog improve his failing grade. She gave him packets of make up work and allowed him to use his notes on certain tests. He managed to pass her class with a C average.

A few weeks prior, just before Christmas, T-Dog's grandmother died. Her battle with kidney disease finally ended because dialysis could do nothing else for her. Ms. Greenley went to her funeral and sat in sorrow as she watched T-Dog cry like an infant. In the weeks proceeding the home going service Ms. Greenley stopped by the house several times with food for T-Dog and his brother.

Now, T-Dog stood face to face with the only teacher who ever cared anything about him and the only girl he ever loved.

"I'm sorry. I'm so sorry, T Dog. I know I shoulda told you. But my momma made me. She made me."

Ms. Greenley looked at Stormy with a confused glare. "What was the girl sorry about? How did these two even know each other?" Ms. Greenley wondered.

Off in the distance Ms. Greenley could hear a swarm of police sirens. She knew they would be at the school within moments. She looked at T-Dog and begged him to let Stormy go.

"She killed my baby, Ms. G! She killed my baby!"

Ms. Greenley raised her eyebrows. She had figured it out. The day before Ms. Greenley administered the EOCT to her ninth grade students, she found Stormy vomiting in the girls bathroom. Stormy begged Ms. Greenley to take her home that afternoon so she wouldn't have to ride the crowded school bus. Ms Greenley obliged. On the ride home Stormy sobbed while telling Ms. Greenley that she thought she was pregnant. Ms. Greenley advised Stormy to talk with her mother immediately. A few days later Ms. Greenley asked Stormy how things were. Stormy said "I'm cool, Ms. G. I finally got over that stomach bug I had the other day".

Now it all made sense. Stormy WAS actually pregnant. Once she told her mother about the child Stormy was forced to have an abortion. She didn't tell Tony until after the procedure was done. The death of his grandmother and the death of his child was too much for Tony to bear. This was the cause of his rage.

"Tony, the police are here. They are gonna shoot you if you don't let Stormy go and give me the gun. You can't get away from them. It's over."

"I ain't goin' back to jail, Ms. G. I ain't goin' back."

T-Dog's voice was calm and determined. He released Stormy's arm. She fell to the floor into Dr.

Fonroy's pool of blood and cried. T-Dog looked at his girlfriend and said, "I love you, baby". He then turned his attention to Ms. Greenley. She was afraid. T-Dog grabbed Ms. Greenley around the waist and squeezed her tightly. She could feel the gun pressing in her back. T-Dog whispered in her ear, "Thanks for taking care of my grandma. And thanks for lookin' out for me. I love you Ms. G."

All the fear left Ms. Greenley's body as she wrapped her arms around T-Dog and returned his embrace. He wiped a tear from his eye and ran out the door into the wooded area behind the school. Ms. Greenley never saw Tony again.

VII

Two months later Ms. Greenley sat in her therapist's office sobbing. She tried to explain her feelings but no words would come out. In fact, she had not spoken to anyone except the police since the incident. Ms. Greenley was lauded as a hero by the school district, her coworkers, and the community. The local news media reported on her heroic act and how she bravely stood up to a "psychopath" . But she felt like a failure.

Her therapist suggested they meet twice a week over the next few months until she showed signs of progression. But Ms. Greenley was not progressing. She suffered from insomnia and grief. Unable to sleep, Ms. Greenley spent most nights watching David Letterman. She would tune in at precisely 11:35 pm to watch the comedian zip across the stage wearing his designer suits and ties. After the hour-long program was over, Ms. Greenley would flip the channels between Jimmy Fallon and reruns of The Andy Griffith show. Ernest T. Bass was the only person who could make her laugh.

Sometimes she would dream about T-Dog. He would stand before her, dressed all in white with his dread locks draped over his shoulders. He'd smile with his perfect teeth and say "What's up, Ms. G?" Then she'd awake in a cold sweat. Ms. Greenley wished she could see him again. But T-Dog was dead. Minutes after the school shooting he was found running down Memorial Drive. The police surrounded him and commanded T-Dog to drop his weapon. T-Dog did not obey. He lifted his gun and aimed it at the officers. Shots were fired and Antonio Cunningham died on the corner of Memorial Drive and Rockbridge Road.

The therapist suggested that journaling could be cathartic for Ms. Greenley. "Writing down your feelings may help you to release them," he told her. The teacher took his advice. She took to journaling with dedication. Every night, usually around 3:00 am Ms. Greenley scribbled in her journal. She wrote about T-Dog, Dr. Fonroy, Zenobia, and Officer Bellows—the four people tragically killed in the incident. There were many students and several staff members injured in the shooting as well. Dr. Moynihan suffered a gunshot wound to her thigh. Jamaica was shot in the arm. Mr. Tarver and a few students had broken bones and minor cuts and scrapes.

There were vigils held at schools and churches in the area. Community leaders held Stop The Violence rallies. And the mayor, governor, state leaders and politicians visited the site to express their condolences.

School resumed three weeks after the shooting occurred. Grief counselors were available for the students and staff members. There was an outpouring of love and support for all involved.

But Ms. Greenley did not return. She couldn't bring herself to go back to her job. Her co-workers managed to pack up her personal belongings and bring them to her home. Ms. Greenley's spirit was in turmoil and she had no idea how she could go on.

She sat and listened to her therapist talk. His words sounded like a mumbled mess. Ms. Greenley wiped her eyes with the crumpled Kleenex and wished for the session to be over. The therapist typed another prescription into the computer and asked Ms. Greenley from what pharmacy she would be picking up her Fluoxetine.

"Panola." she said softly.

Ms. Greenley exited her doctor's office then headed down I-20 towards Panola Road. The rush hour traffic was terrible and Ms. Greenley found herself stuck on the interstate in a long line of cars. Her frustration grew. She opened the sunroof of her SUV and let the sun shine on her face. To pass the time the teacher turned on her radio. It was Friday. Bryan Cameron, V103's afternoon DJ, was on the airways with his crew singing their famous weekend song.

It's Friday! It's Friday!
It's the end of the week and the last day!
Now what you gonna do?
Yo, Bryan, it's on you!

Ms. Greenley smiled and bounced her shoulders to the music. She thought about what she would do this weekend. There was laundry to be done, dishes to be washed and carpet to be vacuumed. She hadn't spoken to any of her friends in nearly two months. They'd call her daily and leave voice messaged on her phone. None of the calls were returned. Many of her friends dropped by and knocked furiously on her door. But she did not answer. Everyone was worried.

At the Panola pharmacy Ms. Greenley dragged herself out of her car and lifted the collar of her raincoat. The sun had hidden behind clouds and it was now raining. The drizzle lightly dusted her hair as she walked swiftly towards the sliding glass door. A small squirrel scurried across the sidewalk avoiding Ms. Greenley's gait. After ordering her medicine she sat in the corner of the room. The theme song from Good Times was playing on the television. It made her smile. It was "The Gang" Ms. Greenley's favorite episode. She watched in amusement as Mad Dog sauntered into the Evans' home in search of JJ. They were going to a gang fight. And JJ, the Evans' oldest son, was forced to go with him. Ms. Greenley sat and stared as Mad Dog pull out his gun and shot JJ as Florida and James, JJ's parents, screamed for help. Ms. Greenley burst into tears. She was unable to control herself. She thought about T-Dog laying on the street bleeding to death after being shot by the police. She thought about Dr. Fonroy's pool of blood that formed at her feet. She thought about Zenobia, shaking in the parking lot. Just as Ms. Greenley stood to make her way to the ladies' restroom she heard her name.

"Christina Greenley!"

Her prescription had been filled. She wiped the snot from her nose and cleaned her hands on her raincoat. Ms. Greenley paid for her medicine then went home and fell asleep in a puddle of her own tears.

VIII

DANITA MOORELAND BEAT VIGOROUSLY ON HER friend's door. It was a rainy April morning and she wanted desperately to stay dry. This routine is one she'd repeated every Saturday since January… drive to Christina Greenley's house, knock on her door, ring her doorbell, and wait. Ms. Greenley had not answered in the past three months. But this day, Danita decided she would not leave until she saw her friend.

Danita held her umbrella tightly and walked around the house to the back door. She stepped in a puddle of water but her rain boots kept her feet dry. Danita knocked on the door and listened. She heard nothing. Thunder reverberated in the sky followed by a bright flash of lightning. She mumbled frustrations under her breath and walked back around to the front of the house. Danita stood on the porch leaning against the brick. She was sad. She knew her friend experienced an awful tragedy. Danita had spent months trying to help Ms. Greenley. But nothing she did was good enough.

A loud clap of thunder sounded above Danita's head and made her jump. Frustrated, she pressed the doorbell then began to knock furiously on the door. To her surprise, she heard the lock shift and saw the doorknob turn. Overjoyed she jumped into her friends embrace and cried. They held each other in the doorway as the thunder rang above their heads.

"I'm so happy to see you. I've missed you so much!"

"I've missed you too," Ms. Greenley whispered with tears in her eyes.

She led her friend to the kitchen where she had just prepared breakfast. Ms. Greenley offered Danita some food. Danita happily accepted and they both sat smiling at one another while eating eggs, grits, and toast.

Once the rain subsided, Danita persuaded Ms. Greenley to get dressed and take a trip to the mall. It would be the first time Ms. Greenley had been shopping since Christmas. Against her better judgment, Ms. Greenley accompanied her friend up interstate 85 towards Buckhead to Lenox Mall.

Danita moved from rack to rack throwing clothing over her shoulders with speed. She disappeared into a dressing room while Ms. Greenley lagged behind. On the third floor of the store, next to women's formal wear, Macy's Department Store displayed some of Gordon Parks' most famous work. The photographs, advertised in white frames, lined the aisles. The pictures stood unnoticed by busy shoppers until Ms. Greenley sauntered by with her hands in her pocket. She stood in front of a photograph of two African-American pilots. They wore leather helmets and sunglasses. These two men, part of the Tuskegee Airmen, looked proud and determined. Ms. Greenley wondered their names. She wondered what their families were like. Were they married? Did they have any children? Sons?

Ms. Greenley's mind began to wander as she stood in front of the Gordon Parks' photographs. Who was T-Dog's father? Did they have a relationship? What would happen to T-Dog's younger brother? Where would he live? Who would take care of him? Ms. Greenley's head began to ache as she turned to find her friend. There stood Danita wearing an orange and green pant suit that was too tight for her body. A pink church hat sat on her head. Danita stood with pride as she held out her hands and yelled "TADDA"! Ms. Greenley forgot about her headache as she buckled over in laughter at her friend.

After a stop at Barnes and Noble, Ms. Greenley slipped into the Apple store to pick up a new case for her iPad. She chose a leopard design with red trim. Danita didn't care much for the case. She claimed it reminded her of The Lion King. This brought on a conversation about Simba's relationship with his "sister" Nahla. The two argued about whether Simba and Nahla were siblings. Danita firmly explained to Ms. Greenley that they were, in fact, siblings because there's only one male per lion pride. Mufasa was the King and all the lioness' were his concubines. Therefore, Simba and Nahla were definitely siblings. The friends laughed hysterically.

Ms. Greenley and Danita followed their hostess to a booth in the corner of California Pizza Kitchen. The eatery was located in the center of Lenox Mall. Due to the open floor plan of the restaurant they had full view of the shops and passers-by. Danita ordered the Chicken Tequila Fettuccine while Ms. Greenley indulged in a pepperoni pizza and garden salad. For dessert, they shared a slice of red velvet cake.

On the drive home Ms. Greenley feel asleep. Even though they only spent a few hours in the mall she was exhausted. It was the most activity Ms. Greenley had participated in over the past few months. The friends hugged goodbye and Danita said she'd call the next day. Ms. Greenley promised to answer the phone.

IX

STONEDALE HIGH SCHOOL'S SENIOR CLASS BUSTLED with pride as they stood admiring one another's graduation caps and gowns, tassels, and honor cords. The girls touched up their make up while the boys straightened their ties and passed around sticks of gum. Throngs of news outlets were dispersed throughout the crowd to capture this moment. Stonedale had suffered a terrible tragedy. But this was a glorious moment which stood as proof that they had ascended from the ashes.

Pomp and Circumstance began to play softly as the crowd stood at attention. Files of graduates marched through the aisles while parents proudly snapped photos. Ms. Greenley stood backstage with her head bowed and eyes closed. She breathed heavily and wondered if she would make it through this day. She pushed all thoughts of T-Dog and Zenobia out of her mind. She dared not think of Dr. Fonroy or Officer Bellows. Just as tears spilled from her face Coach Jordan, the senior class advisor, tapped Ms. Greenley on her back.

"You ready?"

Ms. Greenley shook her head and wiped her eyes. Careful not to trip in her heels, she walked slowly across the stage towards the microphone. Ms. Greenley glanced quickly at her principal, Dr. Moynihan who was seated on the stage beside Mr. Tarver. There were tears in both their eyes. Ms. Greenley, with her head lowered, stood at the podium and breathed heavily. She raised her eyes to the crowd. The graduates stared in amazement at their teacher. No one had seen her since the day of the shooting. It had been four months since the awful event. Ms. Greenley's former students were so relieved to see the teacher they loved. Everyone at the school shared an equal amount of concern about her since she had not returned to work that semester.

Some of the senior girls began to cry. Seeing Ms. Greenley brought back thoughts of that terrible day in January. But they were overjoyed to see the teacher who had meant so much to them. A few of the male graduates stood up and clapped their hands for Ms. Greenley, other's joined in...then others.

Ms. Greenley lifted her eyes from the podium

and felt a sense of bewilderment. This is not the reaction she expected. It reminded her of a scene from one of her favorite movies, Dead Poet's Society. The students, at the end of the movie, stood on their desks in respect for their beloved professor, Mr. Keating, and recited the first line in the Walt Whitman poem, *O Captain, My Captain.*

Hand claps of praise surrounded Ms. Greenley as she turned and saw her principal, assistant principal, co workers and friends all standing in support of her return. She was overwhelmed.

Fumbling with the microphone, Ms. Greenley cleared her throat and began.

If you can keep your head when all about you
Are losing theirs and blaming it on you
If you can trust yourself when all men doubt you
But make allowance for their doubting too
If you can wait and not get tired by waiting
Or being lied about don't deal in lies
Or being hated, don't give way to hating
And yet don't look too good nor talk too wise

If you can dream and not make dreams your master
If you can think and not make thoughts your aim
If you can meet with Triumph and Disaster
And treat those two impostors just the same
If you can bear to hear the truth you've spoken

Twisted by knaves to make a trap for fools,
Or watch the things you gave your life to, broken,
And stoop and build them up with worn-out tools

If you can make one heap of all your winnings
And risk it on one turn of pitch-and-toss
And lose, and start again at your beginnings,
And never breathe a word about your loss,
If you can force your heart and nerve and sinew
To serve your turn long after they are gone,
And so hold on when there is nothing in you
Except the Will which says to them: "Hold on!"

If you can talk with crowds and keep your virtue
Or walk with Kings- nor lose the common touch,
If neither foes nor loving friends can hurt you,
If all men count with you, but none too much
If you can fill the unforgiving minute
With sixty seconds worth of distance run
Yours is the earth and everything in it
And which is more, you'll be a man, my son.

The crowd was silent. Every single person, from the uniformed police officers guarding the doors, to the sound technicians, to the students, was in tears. This poem, written by Rudyard Kipling, was one that Dr. Fonroy quoted at the start of every school day until his death. His voice was heard on the loud speaker in each part of the building reading those words in an attempt to encourage the students. He was a man that was missed. And Ms. Greenley had reminded everyone of his greatness.

X

THE EARLY MORNING SUN CREPT ACROSS THE horizon creating an orange sky. Wind blew through the Atlantic coast causing ripples in the ocean. Ms. Greenley walked along the shore allowing her feet to sink into the wet sand. Myrtle Beach was a beautiful place. She squinted her eyes and looked towards the bright sun. An elderly couple approach Ms. Greenley holding hands, walking their dog. The Jack Russell Terrier sniffed around Ms. Greenley's feet as she smiled at the couple. It was June 13; her birthday.

Ms. Greenley returned to her condo and decided on breakfast. She cracked two eggs in a bowl, poured a drop of milk in, added salt and pepper, then beat the eggs with a fork. She was excited. To celebrate her 28th year she'd attend a John Forte concert that night. Her favorite musician was performing at the

Hard Rock Café on Broadway at the Beach. It would be amazing. This would be her first time seeing the artist in person but she was familiar with his work. She'd followed his career since he produced music with the hip hop group The Fugees. Now, after years in prison for drug possession and a reprieve from President Bush, he had embarked on a new chapter in his life which meant new music, a documentary and numerous tours.

Ms. Greenley opened the envelope that laid on the coffee table of her condo. She eyed her concert ticket. She could not wait to hear John Forte's music that evening. His talent was effortless. His musicianship was exceptional. Ms. Greenley thought his dreadlocks to be breathtakingly beautiful. And his smile gave her chills.

The cell phone laying on a coffee table vibrated repeatedly. Ms. Greenley checked the text messages. She scrolled through a barrage of "Happy Birthday" wishes from her friends and family. This made her smile. Danita left a voice mail stating how sad she was that Ms. Greenley would be spending her birthday alone so far away from her friends. But Ms. Greenley didn't mind. In fact, being in Myrtle Beach, six hours away from her home is just what she wanted. The past few months had been excruciatingly difficult and she felt that coming to Myrtle Beach would help her see things clearer, from a different perspective.

Ms. Greenley laid on the sofa staring at a painting of an overturned beach chair. The chair rested on the ground with sprinkles of sand decorating the top. The ocean rolled in the distance as a surfer navigated its waves. Ms. Greenley tried to read the signature of the painter but was unable to make out his writing. She picked up a novel from the coffee table. The bookmark fell out of the pages and landed on the floor. Ms. Greenley ran her fingers across the top of the book and said aloud, "She's Gone. Kwame Dawes". Ms. Greenley had been reading the book nonstop for the past two days. She was totally enthralled with its characters. Flipping the book over to its back she eyed the author photo. She knew the Jamaican well. As a student at the University of South Carolina Christina Greenley spent many semesters in the front of various seminar English classes taught by the author. He was an associate professor who instructed students on Caribbean literature, African literature, and African-American literature. He was enchanting. Kwame Dawes' heavy Jamaican accent did not deter Ms. Greenley from engulfing every word he spoke. Because of him, she has met extraordinary writers like Kofi Awooner and Colin Channer. As she matriculated through college the student and the professor became friends. She'd sit in his office and listen to his stories about Jamaica, Ghana and his beloved father, Neville. His numerous collections of poetry were all autographed to Ms. Greenley in the similar fashion, "Christina, thanks for everything. One love." It was because of this professor that Ms. Greenley's love of storytellers grew. She became consumed with reading and often spent hours in the University's library searching for new authors.

As she flipped the pages of her friend's novel Ms. Greenley's eyelids became heavy. She tried to awaken herself by blinking fiercely but soon succumbed to sleep with the Jamaican's book laying on her chest.

That afternoon Christina Greenley awoke to the sound of her cell phone ringing. She wiped her eyes and sat up on the couch. Ms. Greenley did not recognize the incoming number but she knew the 803 area code was from South Carolina.

Wondering who would be calling her from her home state, Ms. Greenley cleared her throat and apprehensively answer the phone.

"Hi. Christina Greenley? This is Kenyatta Hull from Palmetto Publishing."

Ms. Greenley's eyebrows rose and she stood up in shock.

"Yes. Hello." Ms. Greenley said softly.

"We received your manuscript and wanted to meet with you to discuss the possibility of publishing it in the near future".

Nothing was said. Ms. Greenley's body fell to the

floor in total disbelief. The Jamaican's book hit the coffee table and landed on the carpet beside its bookmark.

"What did you say?" Ms. Greenley asked with a mixture of fear and confusion.

Kenyatta Hull laughed, then said very slowly, "We loved your novel. And we want to publish it in the fall. Are you available to meet with us next week? We want to fly you to our South Carolina office to discuss a publishing agreement.

"Um....." This is all Ms. Greenley could make out. She was at a loss of words and sat there holding her cell phone to her ear with a sweaty palm. She could not believe the conversation she was having. Ms. Greenley had almost forgotten the weekend that past April where she and Danita drove to the post office and mailed her completed manuscript to several publishing companies. Ms. Greenley had not expected to get a response. Following her therapist's advice, Ms. Greenley has spent the weeks after the school shooting writing about her experience. "It would be cathartic." her therapist said. So she wrote. When she had exhausted every memory of the terrible tragedy Ms. Greenley had produced a 175 page document that she entitled. *Tony's Inferno*. Danita read the story and cried. She was amazed at how Ms. Greenley had so beautifully and accurately given an account of the tragic day's events. "You have to get this published!" Danita demanded. She sat and watched as Danita glued herself to the computer researching various publishing companies. After about an hour Danita immerged with the names, addresses and phone numbers of seven publishers. She even helped Ms. Greenley write a query letter and address all the envelopes. Danita then stuffed her friend in her car along with the envelopes and drove to the post office where they mailed copies of the manuscript.

"Ms. Greenley! Ms. Greenley!" The publisher's voice was agitated. She repeatedly yelled through the phone at the unresponsive teacher.

"Yes, I'm here."

"Do you have a fax number or email address where I can send the contract for you and your agent to look over? We can speak again tomorrow if you have any questions."

Ms. Greenley gave her email address to the publisher. Kenyatta Hull repeated the address for confirmation and thanked her. After the call ended Ms. Greenley remained on the floor listening to the silence at the other end of the phone. She was stunned.

The teacher never imagined she'd be a published author. She had taught English for the past six years and was an avid reader who seldom missed her monthly book club meetings. Since she was in college her favorite past time was perusing the aisle of local book stores in search of new authors and old classics. She loved Shakespeare. She adored Alice Walker. She was obsessed with Nikki Giovanni and Zadie Smith. And now, her book would possibly sit on the shelf beside these favored authors.

The email arrived shortly after their call. Ms. Greenley looked over the contract. The document stated that Palmetto Publishing would publish the manuscript, Tony's Inferno. There was specific language in the contract that mapped out revisions, royalties and distribution. The details were incomprehensible to the teacher so she quickly forwarded the email to her high school friend, LaShonda. Ms. Greenley was confident the Howard Law School graduate would be able to explain the verbiage.

Ms. Greenley's heart raced. She sat on her couch not sure of what she should do next. It was nearly time to prepare for the John Forte concert but she was unable to move. The excitement she felt had her body paralyzed. She tried to slow her breathing and remain calm but it was all too much to bear. Thoughts swam through her mind. She knew Palmetto Publishing to be a reputable company who stood behind their authors and always marketed their writers well. And since Kenyatta Hull's email stated they were interested in further projects from her, Ms. Greenley felt this book deal could be life changing.

Silence abounded the teacher as she remained on the couch trying to regain the use of her limbs. Her hands were numb from immobility and she shook them vigorously to get the blood flowing.

The door of the condo began to shake as a heavy fist knocked furiously. Ms. Greenley jumped. Peering through the peep hole she could see nothing but darkness. Someone's hand was blocking her view. Ms. Greenley nervously asked, "Who is it?" There was laughter. Ms. Greenley put the chain lock on her door and turned the knob. Peaking out of the slightly opened door she saw pink and purple balloons and a cake with white icing.

"Happy Birthday!" the people behind the balloons shouted. Ms. Greenley burst into laughter and unchained her door. Her friends filed in carrying celebration items and presents. Danita, LaShonda and Evette all encircled Ms. Greenley and sang Stevie Wonder's "Happy Birthday" song.

For the next hour the four friends sat in Ms. Greenley's rented beach condo discussing the book deal. There was shared excitement for this new opportunity. Everyone's eyes were wide and smiles were plastered on their faces as they anticipated the impact it could have on Ms. Greenley's life.

"I really appreciate you guys coming to spend my birthday with me." Ms. Greenley told her friends.

"You know we couldn't let you spend an evening

with John Forte without us!" Danita replied.

Ms. Greenley was happy that her friends would join her for the concert. The ladies readied themselves in party-type dresses and MAC cosmetics. As they drove to Broadway on the Beach there were loud bouts of laughter spilling from the car. The group looked stunning as they walked arm in arm through the doors of the Hard Rock Café. Ms. Greenley and her friends sat center stage anxiously anticipating the start of the concert.

XI

THE BLACK EXPEDITION DROVE DOWN GREENE Street toward Longstreet Theater on the campus of The University of South Carolina. Ms. Greenley sat in the back seat glaring out of a tinted window at her alma mater. She hadn't been on the campus in years. The chauffeured car parked in front of Thomas Cooper Library and her driver swiftly opened her door. Ms. Greenley grabbed her attaché case which carried her iPad, a hardcopy of her manuscript, *Tony's Inferno*, and a few Sharpie markers. She smoothed her dress as she stood and walked toward the Russell House.

It was hot. The dry South Carolina heat was dizzying. Beads of sweat formed under Ms. Greenley's armpits as she quickened her pace past a group of street musicians. Inside the Russell House college students rushed to various eateries throughout the building. This was the central location on campus. The student union. The place where everyone convened during lunchtime to grab a bite to eat before their afternoon classes. Ms. Greenley stepped off the elevator onto the third floor. “Gamecock Radio” was displayed in large neon letters above a glass door. A garnet and black sign hung above an adjacent entryway with the words “The Gamecock Newspaper” along its side. Ms. Greenley walked slowly, peering into each office space searching for someone to help her find her way. As she turned down a brightly colored corridor her eyes were met with a drawing of a huge palmetto tree with the words “Palmetto Publishing” painted neatly across the top. Ms. Greenley paused. She adjusted her attaché case from one hand to the other and opened the door.

A potted plant sat on a desk in front of the door. Small specks of soil gathered around the base of the pot. A black Honeywell fan blew cool air, making the plant quiver.

“Hello. Ms. Greenley?” I'm Kenyatta Hull. We spoke on the phone.“

Ms. Greenley shook the hand of the neatly dressed woman and smiled. “Call me, Christina,” she said.

They both sat at the desk with the potted plant

as Kenyatta Hull began to flip through the pages of a garnet and black folder.

"We're glad you're here, Christina. Mr. Thomas is looking forward to seeing you."

"Mr. Thomas?" Ms. Greenley asked.

"Yes," the neatly dressed woman said. "Walter Thomas. He's the new president of Palmetto Publishing. I assumed you knew him."

Ms. Greenley's eyes widened and her eyebrows raised. She knew Walter Thomas well. Seven years ago Christina Greenley was the president of The University of South Carolina's Association of African American Students. Walter Thomas served as the organization's advisor. He worked in the office of Multicultural Student Affairs and had become a strong mentor for many of the Black students on campus.

A tall, muscular gentleman walked towards Ms. Greenley. He was dressed in a gray, Brooks Brother's business suit with a pair of black, newly shined, Stacey Adams shoes. A burgundy ascot peeked from his topcoat. He had one hand in his pocket and offered his free hand to Ms. Greenley.

"Hi, Christina!" he said with a grin.

Ms. Greenley looked up at the man and broke out into a wild smile.

"Walter! I can't believe you're here!" She grabbed him by the neck , giving him a warm embrace. And with a blush, he wrapped his arms around her waist.

Walter escorted Ms. Greenley into his office. He pulled out her chair and motioned for her to have a seat. Walter Thomas sat across from her at a circular table in the corner of his office. A copy of her manuscript sat on the table along with a pile of garnet and black folders. Walter took a sip of tea from his Alpha Phi Alpha engraved glass mug and handed Ms. Greenley one of the folders.

"Look over these documents." Walter said sternly.

He continued sipping his tea as Ms. Greenley fingered the Gamecock symbol that decorated the folder. Looking up at him, Ms. Greenley bit her lip in an attempt to hide her smile.

She recognized the mug. Ms. Greenley had given Walter the mug as a birthday gift many years before. She was 21. He was 25. After she had won the election for the Presidency of The Association of African American Students at The University of South Carolina, Walter, the club advisor, took her and the other elected officers out to celebrate. They went to California Dreaming, a West Columbia restaurant, for dinner. Hours after the other members of her cabinet had made their way back to their dorms, Christina Greenley and Walter Thomas sat on the patio of California Dreaming laughing, talking, and becoming closer. Throughout their conversation Walter touched her wrist repeatedly. Ms. Greenley would rub his palm with her thumb to welcome his advances. He stared at the bridge of her nose and talked of her beauty. She'd blush innocently and look longingly at his lips. By the time Christina Greenley made it back to her off campus apartment Walter had kissed her twice and squeezed the small of her back in a way that made her shiver. For the duration of her senior year Ms. Greenley and Walter Thomas shared a special bond. They managed to keep their relationship a secret. In the presence of others Walter was always careful to treat her as a student and Ms. Greenley always addressed him as her advisor.

On Walter's birthday, three days before Ms. Greenley's college graduation, he confessed his love for her. Christina was thrilled because she had fallen in love with him months prior. She presented him with the engraved glass mug representing his fraternity from which he currently drank. He thanked her for the gift. Walter caressed her cheek, kissed her, and they made love for the first time in the master bedroom of his home.

"You still have the mug," Ms. Greenley said shyly.

"I drink from it every day." he said with a wink.

They both smiled at each other remembering their relationship. After graduation, Ms. Greenley moved to Atlanta to begin her teaching career and enroll in a Master's Degree program at Georgia State University. The time that she and Walter spent together became sporadic and a few months into her first semester of graduate school their relationship ended.

"I've been worried about you," Walter said as he took another sip of his tea.

Ms. Greenley wrinkled her brow and asked why.

Walter answered, "The news. Your school. I've been trying to contact you for months. Then we got your manuscript. As soon as I read the title I knew we would publish it."

"I'm glad you like it." she said.

"Like it? I love it! This is the best thing I've ever read. And I've read *a lot* of books!" Walter exclaimed.

Over the next hour, Ms. Greenley and Walter Thomas talked about their lives during the six years they had been apart. Walter told her the animated details of his rise from Director of Multicultural Affairs at USC to the President of the University's publishing company. As Walter talked, he gently touched Ms. Greenley's wrist as he had done years before. She returned his affection by rubbing his palm with her thumb.

Kenyatta Hull slowly eased her head into the office door. Ms. Greenley and Walter stopped abruptly and glanced toward the entrance.

"So, does Palmetto Publishing have a new author on our team?" Kenyatta asked with a smile.

"Absolutely!" Ms. Greenley said cheerfully.

XII

Black Sharpie markers were strewn about the table. A vase of white lilies sat on top of a white table cloth that kissed the purple carpet. Kenyatta Hull frantically ran around the banquet hall in Booker T. Washington Auditorium wearing a pair of four inch heels that elongated her thin chocolate legs.

Several posters displaying the cover of Ms. Greenley's newly published novel, *Tony's Inferno*, hung throughout the auditorium. Hundred's of hard copies were stacked on a table in the corner of the room. The caterers, wearing white chef's coats, carefully displayed their food platters and serving utensils in the reception area adjacent to the entrance.

In the dressing room, Ms. Greenley twirled around in a full length mirror questioning her attire.

She wore a close fitting cotton pink dress that hugged every inch of her body. The off the shoulder piece accentuated her muscular frame and made her look like a goddess. Walter admired her from across the room.

"Are you sure this is OK?" she wondered aloud.

"It's perfect," Walter answered.

Kenyatta Hull rushed in carrying a notepad and pen. She had a Bluetooth in her ear and spoke quickly to the person on the other line. She spouted a few instructions then ended the conversation.

"Are you ready?" Kenyatta asked with a smile.

Without waiting for an answer, she turned and walked out of the room, expecting the couple to follow.

Ms. Greenley and Walter Thomas walked hand in hand down the hall towards the banquet hall in the Booker T. Washington Auditorium. He spoke softly to her, reassuring the author that the night would be magical. She leaned her head on his shoulder as they walked, finding comfort in his words.

That night, Ms. Greenley gave a rousing 20 minute speech highlighting the dire need of education reform in the public school system. She spoke of the ineffectiveness of high stakes testing, classroom overcrowding, and a need for an increase in teacher salary. The crowd of attendees was in awe of her passion for the education system and the eloquence with which she spoke. They had assembled for a simple book signing. Yet acquired something far greater—a sound understanding of the perils within the public education system and the need for change.

Ms. Greenley autographed one hundred and eighty books that night. She took pictures with old college classmates, reconnected with friends and secured an invitation to provide the keynote address at Voorhees College during their annual Women's Empowerment Conference.

Walter presented Ms. Greenley with a congratulatory bouquet of roses at the end of the evening. He wanted to tell her how much he loved her and how badly he wanted to marry her, but Walter felt it was too soon. They had only rekindled their relationship three months prior. Instead of expounding on his emotional state, Walter simply drove Ms. Greenley to her hotel and kissed her goodnight.

The next morning Ms. Greenley awoke to the sound of an alarm blazing through her room. She slammed her fist on the top of the hotel clock, forcing it to silence.

Today she would be interviewed by Essence Magazine. The publication had selected *Tony's Inferno* as an Essence Book Club honoree.

A short time later Ms. Greenley walked through

the hotel lobby and onto the restaurant patio searching for Walter. He would join her for her interview with the Essence Book Club editor. There were small groups of people scattered throughout the outdoor restaurant enjoying croissants, bagels and omelets. In response to the cool September temperature Ms. Greenley stood at the entrance wearing a simple black dress with a gray cardigan and a pair of ballet flats. A soft wind blew through the patio just as Ms. Greenley felt a hand wrap around her waist from behind. Without looking back she smiled while Walter kissed the back of her neck.

"Good morning," he said softly.

Ms. Greenley turned slowly and kissed his cheek. The couple seated themselves at a white linen table in the center of the restaurant. Walter reviewed a few talking points with the author as they waited for the magazine editor.

Daphne Richards arrived and introduced herself to the couple. She sat at their table and spread her accoutrements across the white linen. With a frazzled look on her face, the editor, very business-like, quickly began her line of questioning. Ms. Greenley quietly answered each question, expounding on her inspiration for writing the novel. She talked about her school, her years of experience, and her relationship with the shooter. Ms. Greenley swallowed hard as she recalled that January afternoon when her life changed. She fought back tears as she remembered the many lives that were lost.

Although the conversation was being recorded, Daphne took furious notes as Ms. Greenley talked. Walter sat quietly, listening to the interview. He gently touched Ms. Greenley's knee under the table to calm her when her voice quivered. She found great comfort in this.

The interview ended with handshakes and thank-yous. Daphne Richards exited the patio restaurant, leaving Walter and Ms. Greenley alone. Their time was limited because Ms. Greenley would be returning to Atlanta that afternoon. Walter was sad to see her go, but took solace in knowing that it wouldn't be long before they saw each other again. The couple enjoyed breakfast together then made their way to the airport.

XIII

ON A CHILLY OCTOBER MORNING MS. GREENLEY'S sophomore honors English class filed quietly into the room. She stood at the door greeting her students. Their daily warm up exercise was displayed on the Promethean board in the front of the class. Today they would begin a lesson on The Great Depression era. This lesson would serve as an introduction to their class novel, Of Mice and Men. As the students worked Ms. Greenley took attendance then walked around the room to ensure each person was on task.

This semester proved to be less stressful, unlike previous semesters Ms. Greenley had taught. Because of the tragedy that she witnessed last year her principal, Dr. Moynihan, decided to give her a less challenging teaching schedule. Ms. Greenley taught two senior honors English classes and one sophomore honors class. She had no more than fifteen students in each period. Ms. Greenley was also given a fourth period planning to allow time for her to meet with her therapist at the end of the work day. The therapist still required weekly meetings because Ms. Greenley needed to be closely monitored while taking Fluoxetine for anxiety and depression.

Ms. Greenley gave each student a study guide for the novel and began a brief lecture on migrant workers in America during the 1930's. The students asked thought provoking questions about World War II, poverty, and President Franklin D. Roosevelt. After the mini lesson, the students were separated into groups and given one of several tasks. Group 1 labeled a map by identifying a list of cities and landforms in California concentrating on the areas located near Soledad, the novel's setting. Group 2 completed a word analysis of several vocabulary terms found in the first chapter. The third group was responsible for reading short bios of John Steinbeck, the book's author and Ernest Hemingway. Then they had to compare the two authors using a Venn diagram.

With ten minutes remaining in the class period, Ms. Greenley assembled the students back together and read the poem "To a Mouse, on Turning Her Up in Her Nest with a Plough" by Robert Burns. The teacher explained that John Steinbeck used this poem as his inspiration for the title of *Of Mice and Men*. Their homework, Ms. Greenley told them, was to analyze the poem and identify its theme. The bell sounded and the students filed out of the class yelling a round of "Bye, Ms. G. See you tomorrow!"

During her planning period, Ms. Greenley headed towards the front office to check her mailbox. She walked with her head down as to avoid eye contact with any students or staff members. Ms. Greenley was sad. The reminders of the school shooting were still fresh in her memory and it pained her to come to work each day. As she walked she thought about Dr. Fonroy, Zenobia, and Officer Bellows. She stared at the white tiled floors and imagined their spilled blood gathering around her feet. Ms. Greenley stopped. She watched the puddle of blood grow bigger and bigger. Ms. Greenley tried to move but her feet were stuck to the floor. She was trapped. Her heart began to race as she searched for an escape. Just as the teacher opened her mouth to scream for help Lionel Superion walked towards her with a broom in his hand and a trash bag tied around his head.

"Hello purdy lady. I sure want ta take you bak to de island wit me."

Coming out of her trance she looked up at the custodian with relief. He was a sight to see. His gold tooth shined brightly in Ms. Greenley's eyes and the trash bag made a noise each time he moved his head.

"I told you before. It's too hot in Jamaica."

Picking her feet up from the tiled floor Ms. Greenley turned and abruptly walked away.

Stonedale High School's front office was unusually quiet. Ms. Cody, the attendance secretary typed furiously on her computer. There was a smell of cigarette smoke encircling Ms. Cody that made Ms. Greenley frown as she passed.

Mr. Tarver stood at the Xerox machine making copies for his afternoon meeting.

"Hey, I just saw your article in Essence. You gonna be famous, girl!"

"I'd rather win the lottery," Ms. Greenley joked.

Hearing Ms. Greenley's voice Dr. Moynihan called out, "Ms. G., step into my office please." Ms. Greenley stepped into the dimly lit office and admired the purple walls. A beautiful bouquet of purple hydrangeas sat in a glass vase that was positioned in the middle of a circular table. To Ms. Greenley's surprise stacks of her novel, *Tony's Inferno*, laid on the table beside the vase.

Dr. Moynihan held up the latest issue of Essence magazine and smiled. She waved it from side to side and began to dance around her desk. This made Ms. Greenley chuckle.

"We are so proud of you," Dr. Moynihan said once she discontinued her dance. "This is a wonderful interview. I think of Tony often. I wish there was something more we could have done to help him."

"This is a terrible world we live in." Ms. Greenley said as she lowered her eyes.

"So many people in pain and not knowing how to deal with their hurt."

Both women looked down at the floor reflecting on the tragic school shooting. There was a stillness in the room—an impromptu moment of silence for all those affected by the killings.

Attempting to lighten the mood in her office Dr. Moynihan walked to the table and pointed at the stack of books.

"Are you gonna sign these things or what?"

"Of course I'll sign them. Where did they all come from?"

"The district ordered them."

Ms. Greenley raised her eyebrows in shock. "For the whole school?" she asked.

"No. for the entire county. Every teacher in Dent County will receive one of your books." The district mandated that we use it for staff development at our next training session.

"Every teacher!!?? That's over 10,000 books!"

"Yes! It is," Dr. Moynihan laughed. "I assumed the Superintendent notified you last week."

"Well, I was out last week. If you'll remember I was away giving a talk at an education conference at

Benedict College."

"Oh, Yes." Dr. Moynihan said. "I remember. I hope it went well."

Not giving time for Ms. Greenley to answer Dr. Moynihan asked if the teacher would autograph as many books as she could before the end of the school day. There was a staff meeting that afternoon and the books would be passed out then. Ms. Greenley sat in shock and autographed all one hundred and thirty seven novels for her co-workers. As she scribbled her name she tried to comprehend what an order of 10,000 books would mean to her future. Ms. Greenley was excited. And she couldn't stop smiling.

XIV

There were two things that Ms. Greenley loved about her job: seeing her students progress throughout the school year, and the many holiday breaks the district had on its calendar. It was Thanksgiving and school was closed. Ms. Greenley had an entire week to spend with family and friends.

This year, instead of going to north Georgia to her aunt's home, she opted to have Thanksgiving dinner with Walter and his family. They traveled to Sumter, South Carolina early Thursday morning and made it just in time to see the start of the Thanksgiving Day Parade, hosted by Morris College. The grand marshal rode down North Main Street atop a black Cadillac convertible waving proudly to the crowd. The onlookers met his greeting with bright smiles and warm hand waves of their own.

Ms. Greenley sat in a blue lawn chair with her legs crossed and her arms folded to protect her body from the cold. Her brown knee-high boots had small drops of mud on the bottom. Candace Thomas, Walter's sister, sat beside Ms. Greenley in a matching blue lawn chair. They both chatted intently and laughed at the hysterics of the crowd.

The Manning High School marching band stopped in front of the group of onlookers. The drum line beat furiously on their instruments, causing vibrations in the air. Their routine made the crowd clap their hands and run into the street to dance. This was a sight to see—a wonderful celebration of a community.

The exhibition down North Main Street drew thousands of spectators. Walter's entire family was assembled on the front lawn of his mother's house enjoying the festivities. Ms. Greenley, though not an official member of the family, felt at ease and at home. For the first time in a very long time, she was comfortable, happy, and unafraid.

The Thanksgiving dinner festivities lasted long into the night. Ms. Greenley and Walter stuffed themselves on rice, greens, chicken, ham, smothered pork chops, corn bread, rolls, and sweet potato pie. After dinner, Walter and his sisters made an attempt to teach Ms. Greenley how to play spades. She and Walter were partners but after the first round they were one hundred and sixty points behind. So, Ms. Greenley decided to join the children in a game of Candy Land.

Shortly after midnight, Walter drove Ms. Greenley back to his home in Columbia. As they entered the subdivision Ms. Greenley opened her tired eyes. She stared at large black letters sitting on a brick wall. "The Summit" she said aloud. Ms. Greenley watched as the man-made waterfall poured over the letters spilling into a pool.

"We're home!" she said jokingly as she stretched her arms.

Slowly, Walter glanced at her. He rubbed his finger down the bridge of her nose and smiled. Fighting the fear that welled in his throat. Walter opened his mouth and with a deep breath said, "I love you."

He breathed a sigh of relief. These are the words he had wanted to tell Ms. Greenley since the day she walked into Palmetto Publishing for their first meeting. He felt a rush of emotion. And desperately tried to fight back tears. He turned into the driveway of his home on Amaryllis Trail and let up the garage door. Ms. Greenley grabbed Walter's free hand and squeezed.

"I love you, too." she said softly.

The next morning Ms. Greenley awoke to the smell of bacon. She laid in bed and listened to pots rattle in the kitchen. Her heart beat quickly as she thought about the previous night. Ms. Greenley was elated that Walter confessed his love for her. She had wanted to tell him her feelings for months but was afraid. Now, she was free to express herself to Walter. This would prove to be a turning point in their relationship.

Ms. Greenley readied herself for the day and descended from the upstairs guest room into the kitchen. Two place settings were neatly prepared at the table. Walter poured orange juice into a glass and handed it to his love.

"Good morning, beautiful," he said cheerfully.

"Good morning, Mr. Thomas," Ms. Greenley said with a smile.

"You know," Walter began to say, "Christina Thomas sounds much better than Christina Greenley..."

Ms. Greenley looked up at Walter and bit her bottom lip, hiding her smile. "You think so?" she asked. With a quiet chuckle, Walter winked his eye at her and continued scrambling eggs.

The drive to the airport was quiet. Their Thanksgiving holiday was enjoyable and neither Ms. Greenley, nor Walter wanted it to end; but she had to go home and prepare her students for End of

Coarse Testing at Stonedale High.

They walked hand in hand through the airport towards the security checkpoint. Stopping short of the gate, Walter turned to Ms. Greenley and kissed her.

"Do you ever think about...."

"About what?" Ms. Greenley asked.

"....getting married." Walter said shyly.

Ms. Greenley looked down at the floor and shuffled her feet.

"Sometimes." she admitted.

"Well, I think we should get married. I mean, I... I want to be with you. I...I want you to be my wife."

Ms. Greenley breathed heavily without knowing how to respond. She opened her mouth to say something but was unable to form any words.

Walter continued, "Do you think we should....get married?"

"...... um, well, I don't know...I um. I mean, I love you...I just..... I don't know."

Ms. Greenley knew exactly what she wanted to say. She wanted to jump into Walter's arms and scream out "YES! I absolutely think we should get married!" But she was afraid. And she didn't feel like a busy airport was the appropriate place to discuss such an important topic.

"Let's talk about this when I get home. I'll call you after my flight. I love you."

Ms. Greenley hugged Walter goodbye, kissed him softly, and walked towards the security check point without looking back.

XV

THE $86,000.00 CHECK SAT ON MS. GREENLEY'S coffee table in her living room. She stared at it. Stunned. Afraid to touch it. The numbers seemed to dance in the air while the paper glowed. *Tony's Inferno* had proven to be a huge success. With the Essence interview, the feature in Huffington Post, a nomination for the Library of Congress' new writer's award and various college appearances, Ms. Greenley's first book was gaining momentum. She was excited, but not quite sure what to make of this profit. This $86,000.00 check from Palmetto Publishing was more than she could earn in two years through teaching. Ms. Greenley didn't know what to do. She wanted desperately to call Walter but he was traveling to the International Publishers Congress in Bangkok, Thailand and would be unavailable until the next evening. She sat up on her sofa and stared at the check. She counted the number of zeros. There were so many! She checked her name to be sure it was spelled correctly. Ms. Greenley laid back on her sofa and closed her eyes. She imagined the many things she could do with the funds. There were no student loans to speak of because due to her academic success in high school she had been awarded a Gates Millennium Scholarship. This award would cover her undergraduate and graduate school tuitions. Just as she began to think of a much needed vacation to Hawaii, Ms. Greenley remembered the stacks and stacks of student essays that needed grading. Grudgingly, she spent the next two hours on her couch grading papers and glancing in disbelief at the $86,000.00 check.

The next week was long and tedious. The school was immersed in End of Course Testing. All the students were frazzled because of the pressures placed upon them to do exceedingly well on the battery of tests. And the teachers did their best to follow proper rules and procedures due to the various allegations of cheating throughout the district in years prior.

The week proved to be a smooth one, with the exception of a brief loss of power in the ninth grade academy. Ms. Greenley students, and all others effected by the power outage were required to fill out an incident report which gave them the option to retake the test at a later date.

As Ms. Greenley walked into the assistant principal's office to return her testing booklets she remembered Dr. Fonroy. His office was now occupied by a new administrator, Ms. Peoples, but not much had changed. Ms. Greenley looked at his desk, his chair, his computer. She thought about his glasses that lay sideways on his face while he lay in his own pool of blood. She thought about his cell phone that she pulled out of his pocket to call emergency services. Ms. Greenley's heart began to race as she struggled for breath. She grabbed her chest and looked around for help. Her throat tightened, preventing her from calling out to someone.

"Ms. Greenley!"

There was a tug on her arm. The panicked teacher turned and saw Mr. Tarver. He took her testing documents and placed them on a table then escorted her out of the office. They walked slowly down the hall away from the memories, arm in arm, sobbing.

Back in Mr. Tarver's office Ms. Greenley sat on a red leather couch that was worn in many places. The assistant principal wiped his eyes with tissue and shuffled his feet on the floor.

"I think this might be my last year, Ms. G. I can't do this anymore. I miss my friend."

"I know. I miss him too. I miss everybody. It's just so sad around here. I can barely sleep at night." Ms. Greenley admitted.

"I've been taking sleeping pills for almost a year, Ms. G. But they don't help. I still can't sleep."

The two spent the next half hour consoling one another and talking about the lives that were lost. It made them both feel better to share their pain with someone else who experienced the same tragedy.

That night Ms. Greenley laid in bed and thought about what Mr. Tarver told her. She too, felt that she would not be able to complete another year of teaching. Ms. Greenley wanted desperately to resign from her position but she had no idea what she would do to replace her income. The teacher wanted nothing more to do with the education system. She had been devastated by the tragedy and seemed unable to recover. Her therapist wanted to increase her medication but Ms. Greenley refused. They were still meeting once a week and most sessions left Ms. Greenley in tears.

Since the school shooting, the teacher has lost 20 lbs and still struggled to make it through a day without hallucinations or an anxiety attack. Walter had a way of calming her, but since they lived in different states, Ms. Greenley day to day life was a struggle.

She turned in her bed and looked at her clock. It

was 1:45 am. Ms. Greenley closed her eyes tightly and tried to force herself to sleep. She knew that if she didn't sleep that night she'd suffer with a terrible headache the next day and wanted to avoid it at all costs.

"What's up, Ms. G?"

Ms. Greenley opened her eyes. T-Dog stood at her bedside smiling, exposing his perfect teeth. She stared at his broad nose and silky dreadlocks hanging over his shoulder.

"Hey, Tony." she said softly.

"I miss you Ms. G. I'm sorry about all the trouble I caused. I ain't mean to hurt nobody."

"I know, Tony. I'm sorry I couldn't help you."

A sharp pain jilted Ms. Greenley's side. She jumped out of her bed in complete fear and astonishment. Her back was wet with sweat. She looked around the room for Tony. She was alone. Her bedroom was quiet. The automated heating unit clicked in her hallway and she felt a warm rush of air from her overhead vent. Ms. Greenley glared at her clock. It was 5:15 am. She had been dreaming. Her head pounded and her eyes filled with tears. The teacher sat on the side of her bed and buried her head in her hands.

It was difficult to make it to work that morning, but the Christmas holidays were fast approaching and Ms. Greenley didn't want to miss any days so close to a vacation. The teacher spend her school day conferencing with each of her students concerning grades and their impending final exams. To make it through her workday, Ms. Greenley took several aspirin. Her headache had gotten worse as the day progressed so during her fourth period planning, she locked her classroom door, turned off her light, and rested her head on her desk.

XVI

Saturday morning Ms. Greenley awoke to the sound of wind beating against her window. It was cloudy and the temperature was nearly freezing. She wrapped herself tightly in her blanket and turned on the television to watch The Melissa Harris Perry Show on MSNBC.

This week the panel of experts focused on increasing college tuition prices and the need for education reform. Georgetown University professor, Michael Eric Dyson, waxed poetic about the inequality and ineffectiveness of high stakes testing in the public school system which placed students of color at a disadvantage. Ms. Greenley watched the lively discussion and pondered many themes that were analyzed by the guests.

She thought the host to be amazing. Ms. Greenley

had long admired Melissa Harris Perry since the liberal political commentator was a professor at Tulane University. Ms. Greenley had read all of her books and was thrilled to learn that the professor would host a show on MSNBC.

Ms. Greenley thought back to last February, shortly after the tragedy, when she had an opportunity to hear a lecture by Melissa Harris Perry at Spelman College. Ms. Greenley sat in the front row of the Cosby Academic Center Auditorium shuffling nervously in her seat. She had arrived hours early to ensure she'd be able to hear her mentor speak. Melissa Harris Perry did not disappoint. The professor eloquently delivered a talk on Women's Struggle for Full Citizenship and the importance that the education of young girls played in the progression of America.

After the lecture, Ms. Greenley cautiously made her way to the podium and with tears in her eyes, told Melissa Harris Perry that she was her hero. The professor thanked her and hugged her lovingly.

Once the two hour news program ended, Ms. Greenley turned off her television and listened to the silence that surrounded her. A small tear fell from her eyes onto her while linen pillowcase. And then another. And another. Ms. Greenley cried herself back to sleep and dreamed about Tony, Zenobia, Officer Bellows, and Dr. Fonroy.

That afternoon Ms. Greenley found herself at the post office. She stuffed her resignation forms in an envelope, sealed it closed, and dropped it into the mail box. It was done. Ms. Greenley had officially resigned from Dent County School System. As she sat in her car gripping her steering wheel, Ms. Greenley breathed heavily. She felt a sense of relief and a deep, deep sadness. She loved teaching. She loved her students. But the stresses of her job were too much. The student's lack of motivation, their behavior, their parents; the paperwork, the politics, the high-stakes testing, the unreasonable amount of pressure placed on teachers to perform miracles in the classroom; the weight of it all was too much for Ms. Greenley to bear any longer.

And then there was Tony. After nearly a year, Ms. Greenley had not been able to return to her former self. She was still having panic attacks and frequent hallucinations. She dreamed of Tony regularly. She had trouble sleeping. So this resignation, while undesired, was necessary.

For the remainder of the weekend, Ms. Greenley thought of ways she would tell her boss, Dr. Moynihan, what she had done. The teacher knew that Dr. Moynihan would not be pleased with her decision and the Principal would be very upset to have to scramble to find a replacement after the Christmas holiday.

On Monday morning, Ms. Greenley bravely marched into the front office of Stonedale High School. She loosened the scarf that was tied around her neck and removed her gloves. Ms. Greenley greeted Mr. Tarver and asked if Dr. Moynihan had arrived.

"She's here. Already on cafeteria duty," Mr. Tarver stated.

Ms. Greenley thanked her friend and proceeded to the cafeteria. There was mass confusion as the students scrambled to various breakfast lines. Ms. Greenley weaved in and out of the crowd dodging hyperactive teenagers who were oblivious to their surroundings. She searched for the school's principal but could not find her amid the chaos. The morning bell rang, signifying the start of the school day. Out of time, Ms. Greenley gave up her search and made her way to her classroom in the ninth grade academy.

By the end of the day Ms. Greenley had made many attempts to speak to her boss. But with the food fight in the cafeteria, the false fire alarm, and a surprise visit to the school by the new superintendent, Dr. Moynihan had no time to talk with Ms. Greenley. It wasn't until that afternoon, well after the end of the school day, when the two finally saw one another. Dr. Moynihan was in the school parking lot packing her car with boxes from the school cookie dough fundraiser. Ms. Greenley walked over to the white BMW.

"Hi, Dr. Moynihan."

Dr. Moynihan's head emerged from the trunk of her car. She looked at Ms. Greenley and smiled.

"Hey. I heard you were looking for me."

As Ms. Greenley gave her boss the news Dr. Moynihan's eyes lowered to the ground. She took several deep breaths as she listened to Ms. Greenley explain her reasons for resigning. When Ms. Greenley was done giving her well-rehearsed speech the principal looked up at her with tear filled eyes. Dr. Moynihan grabbed Ms. Greenley's hand and squeezed. To Ms. Greenley's surprise, Dr. Moynihan began telling her how her life had changed over the past year. She talked of her restless nights, lack of appetite, and fear that there would be another school shooting at Stonedale High. She told Ms. Greenley how much she missed Dr. Fonroy and how sad she was for the families of the people who died. Dr. Moynihan went on to say she thought Ms. Greenley to be very brave for attempting to come back another year. The principal told her teacher how proud she was of the work that Ms. Greenley had done at the school and how badly she wanted her to stay. With a heartfelt embrace the two women ended their conversation and went separate ways, still in tears.

Over the next two days Ms. Greenley monitored

her students while they took their semester exams. Her classroom was peaceful and pleasant as the children vigorously bubbled in answers and composed essay responses on their test documents. After grading the stack of exam papers and finalizing the grades for each class Ms. Greenley's attention turned to cleaning her classroom. She spent a few hours after school purging all unnecessary papers and materials from her file cabinet and closet.

It was an emotional day. Ms. Greenley stood in the center of her empty classroom and breathed heavily. This is the room she had spent many years in and it saddened her to know that her time there would soon end. The teacher was unsure of what she'd do next, but she knew she wanted peace. She knew she wanted joy to return to her life.

She looked at a poster of *The Cask of Amontillado* laying alone on a table. She thought about the main character of the story, Fortunado. What an unlucky life he had! His friend, Montresor, was so hideous and cruel. How could Montresor commit such an awful deed? How could he be so methodical, manipulating, maniacal? How could he be filled with such hate to chain his friend to a wall and enclose the door of the wall with bricks, trapping his friend inside?

Ms. Greenley stood in the empty classroom watching Montresor's bricks form around her. She was underground in the catacombs, chained to the wall just as Fortunado had been. Montresor laughed hysterically at her pleas to be released. She was trapped. Ms. Greenley tried to break free of the chains but it was too late. Montresor had put the last brick in place. She was walled in, unable to escape. The niter was taking hold of Ms. Greenley's throat. She struggled to breathe. She felt the poison seeping into her lungs. She battled with the chains around her wrists as she broke into tears. Ms. Greenley exerted all her energy in an attempt to break free. Just as she had succumbed to defeat she felt a hand on her shoulder. Ms. Greenley screamed violently and turned her body around in shock. There stood Jamaica with a trash bag tied around his head.

"Hello purdy lady. I didn't mean ta scare ya like dat."

Sweaty, exhausted, and confused, Ms. Greenley ran out of the room in tears.

XVII

ON FRIDAY MORNING, THE DAY BEFORE CHRISTMAS break, Ms. Greenley rushed to the grocery store bakery to pick up the red velvet cupcakes she had ordered. It was her last day of work and she thought she'd reward her students for their diligence throughout the semester. She strolled through the sports drink aisle and threw a few packs of Capri Sun juice boxes in her cart along with decorative Christmas napkins and a breakfast bagel.

After loading her trunk with the purchased items Ms. Greenley cranked her SUV and bit into her bagel. It was stale. The clock read 7:45 am. She had fifteen minutes to get to work. The teacher sped down Memorial Drive and quickly made a left on Central Avenue. Throngs of students lined the sidewalks on their way to school. Mr. Tarver stood at the bus entrance and waved vigorously at Ms. Greenley as she parked her car in the teacher parking lot. Dr. Moynihan's white BMW was parked in the adjacent space and Ms. Greenley was careful not to hit it as she unloaded her treats.

"Dere's mi gurl! Hello purdy lady!"

Jamaica strolled towards Ms. Greenley wearing a red polo shirt with a Stonedale High School Pirate emblem and freshly ironed khaki pants. Ms. Greenley was stunned. There was no trash bag around his head and he sported a fresh haircut and shave.

Aware of her shock, Jamaica proclaimed, " I decided ta dress nice for you, my love. Since dis is yer last day en all."

"You look wonderful, Jamaica. Thank you so much. I'm gonna miss you."

The custodian grabbed Ms. Greenley's hand and gently said, "Don't go, mi lady. I gon tek ya to de island wit me."

"It's too hot in Jamaica!" Ms. Greenley exclaimed.

The co-workers laughed hysterically and gave one another a kind-hearted hug. Jamaica assisted Ms. Greenley with her packages and she rewarded him with a red velvet cupcake that he wasted no time eating.

Throughout the day each of her classes showed appreciation for her treats. They sat in silence eating their cupcakes and juice while watching Anonymous, a movie about the conspiracy surrounding William Shakespeare's writings. It was a nice end to a very long semester.

As the bell sounded to mark the beginning of Ms. Greenley's fourth period planning Mr. Tarver's voice came on the loud speaker.

"Please pardon the interruption. May I have your attention for a very important announcement?"

And then there was silence. For well over a minute the school listened to the shuffling of the microphone and someone repeatedly clearing his throat. Ms. Greenley stood at her door with a furrowed brow wondering what was happening in the school's office.

"Christina Greenley," the voice began, "you are my world. I'm so thankful that we have reconnected after all these years apart."

Ms. Greenley raised her eyebrows. It was Walter. What was he doing at her school? What was this announcement about? She walked to the speaker hanging on the wall in her empty classroom to hear his voice clearer.

"You are my closet friend and my trusted confidant. I don't want to ever be apart from you. I'm happiest when you are around and your smile makes my heart skip a beat. You are beautiful. Wonderful. Perfect. A gift from God . And I want nothing more than to make you my wife. Christina, please say you'll marry me."

Ms. Greenley's mouth hung open as she clenched her chest. Her tear filled face stared up at the speaker hanging on the wall in disbelief. She did not move.

With another shuffling of the microphone Mr. Tarver's voice said, "Ms. Greenley, please report to the front office."

She tentatively opened her classroom door. In the hallway, rows and rows of students and teachers had gathered. They were clapping and smiling from ear to ear. Ms. Greenley quickened her pace as she wiped her tears and laughed at the assembly. Her students waved and cheered as their teacher passed. Ms. Greenley rounded the corner and entered the attendance office where Ms. Cody and a host of other staff members stood cheering. Mr. Tarver and Dr. Moynihan hugged Ms. Greenley and guided her to the main entryway where Walter knelt holding a jewelry box. The teacher could not stop the river of tears that fell as Walter grabbed her hand.

"Will you marry me?" he said gently. Ms. Greenley, overcome with unspeakable joy, fell into Walter's arms and cried "Yes!" There was a roar of cheers from the office staff. Mr. Tarver cleared his throat and spoke into the microphone to alert the school, "She said yes!" Every student, teacher, and staff member at Stonedale High School erupted in applause for Ms. G.

Acknowledgements

Each day, when I came home from school I'd sit and listen to my mom and dad tell stories about the daily exploits in their classrooms. As each of my sister's graduated from college and became teachers, they too, got a chance to become a part of the conversation. I wanted nothing more than to grow up and be able to have my own stories to tell. Now, at each family function, we all sit and discuss the good and bad of our daily work in education. I'm so grateful for growing up in a house filled with educators. I thank my parents for sharing their love of teaching with me. And I thank my four sisters for giving me encouragement to get through each day.

To my most memorable teachers- Ms. Alphene Colclough, Dr. Kwame Dawes, Dr. Dianne Johnson-Feelings, and Dr. Cleveland Sellers- thank you for the years of work you've done to bring about change in the world. You made me love learning.

To my students- the good, the bad, the obedient, the challenging, the kind, the cruel- you all kept me on my toes and made each workday quite an adventure. I hope I was able to impart knowledge and bring a little more joy into your lives.

To my husband- you are more than I could have every prayed for. I thank God for thinking enough of me to put you in my life as my provider, comforter, confidant and friend. You are amazing. Thank you for believing that I can fly.

To my children- you have given me purpose. This book serves as proof that you must always push fear aside and follow your dreams. Mommy loves you. Thank you for giving me time to write.

www.ingramcontent.com/pod-product-compliance
Lightning Source LLC
LaVergne TN
LVHW091011080826
845145LV00003B/1223